Dear Parent:
Your child's love of reading starts here!

Every child learns to read in a different way and at his or her own speed. Some go back and forth between reading levels and read favorite books again and again. Others read through each level in order. You can help your young reader improve and become more confident by encouraging his or her own interests and abilities. From books your child reads with you to the first books he or she reads alone, there are I Can Read Books for every stage of reading:

SHARED READING
Basic language, word repetition, and whimsical illustrations, ideal for sharing with your emergent reader

BEGINNING READING
Short sentences, familiar words, and simple concepts for children eager to read on their own

READING WITH HELP
Engaging stories, longer sentences, and language play for developing readers

READING ALONE
Complex plots, challenging vocabulary, and high-interest topics for the independent reader

ADVANCED READING
Short paragraphs, chapters, and exciting themes for the perfect bridge to chapter books

I Can Read Books have introduced children to the joy of reading since 1957. Featuring award-winning authors and illustrators and a fabulous cast of beloved characters, I Can Read Books set the standard for beginning readers.

A lifetime of discovery begins with the magical words "I Can Read!"

Visit www.icanread.com for information
on enriching your child's reading experience.

WALT DISNEY PICTURES AND WALDEN MEDIA PRESENT "THE CHRONICLES OF NARNIA: THE LION, THE WITCH AND THE WARDROBE" BASED ON THE BOOK BY C.S. LEWIS
A MARK JOHNSON PRODUCTION AN ANDREW ADAMSON FILM MUSIC COMPOSED BY HARRY GREGSON-WILLIAMS COSTUME DESIGNER ISIS MUSSENDEN EDITED BY SIM EVAN-JONES PRODUCTION DESIGNER ROGER FORD
DIRECTOR OF PHOTOGRAPHY DONALD M. McALPINE, ASC, ACS CO-PRODUCER DOUGLAS GRESHAM EXECUTIVE PRODUCERS ANDREW ADAMSON PERRY MOORE
WALDEN MEDIA SCREENPLAY BY ANN PEACOCK AND ANDREW ADAMSON AND CHRISTOPHER MARKUS & STEPHEN McFEELY PRODUCED BY MARK JOHNSON PHILIP STEUER DIRECTED BY ANDREW ADAMSON Walt Disney Pictures

Distributed by BUENA VISTA PICTURES DISTRIBUTION THE CHRONICLES OF NARNIA, NARNIA, and all book titles, characters and locales original therein are trademarks of C.S. Lewis Pte Ltd. and are used with permission. ©Disney Enterprises, Inc. and Walden Media, LLC. All rights reserved.

Narnia.com

❖

THE CHRONICLES OF NARNIA
THE LION, THE WITCH AND THE WARDROBE
TEA WITH MR. TUMNUS

Adapted by Jennifer Frantz

Based on the screenplay by
Ann Peacock and Andrew Adamson and
Christopher Markus & Stephen McFeely

Based on the book by C. S. Lewis

Directed by Andrew Adamson

HarperCollins*Publishers*

"Ninety-four . . . ninety-five . . ."
Lucy's oldest brother, Peter, was counting.
They were playing hide-and-seek.
Lucy needed a place to hide before
he got to one hundred!

"Ninety-six . . . ninety-seven . . . ,"
Peter counted.
Lucy dashed into a room and
jumped into an old wardrobe.

Inside, the wardrobe smelled like mothballs.
Some old fur coats tickled Lucy's arm.
She reached for the back of the wardrobe
with her hand.
Lucy felt a gust of cold air.

Where could that be coming from?
Lucy thought.
She stepped forward and felt snow
crunching beneath her feet.
Lucy was not in the wardrobe any longer.

She was outside in a forest!
Lucy saw a lamppost glowing warmly
in the wintry, overcast weather.

As Lucy got closer to the lamppost,
something near her moved!
Lucy turned and screamed.

The strange creature in front
of her screamed, too.
It was just as surprised as Lucy!

"I am sorry," Lucy said.
"I hope I did not scare you."
"Most certainly not," the creature replied.
"Though you are odd-looking for a Dwarf."

"I am not a Dwarf!" Lucy said.
"I am a *girl*!"

The creature looked shocked.

"You are a ... *Human*?" it asked.

"Yes!" Lucy replied.

"My name is Lucy Pevensie.

And what, may I ask, are you?"

"I am a Faun.
My name is Tumnus,"
he said, and put out his hand.
Lucy smiled and shook Mr. Tumnus's hand.

"Lucy Pevensie," Mr. Tumnus said.
"How would it be if you came
and had tea with me?"

Lucy knew she should get home soon,
but she was curious about her new friend.
"All right," Lucy replied.
"I suppose I could come for a little while."

Lucy and Mr. Tumnus walked
through the snow together.

He told Lucy that she was in Narnia.
"Is it always this cold in Narnia?"
Lucy asked.
"It has been this way for the last one hundred
years," Mr. Tumnus said sadly.

Lucy and Mr. Tumnus reached
his cozy little cottage.
Inside, it was warm and filled with books.
Lucy forgot all about the coldness outside.

Mr. Tumnus fixed tea and toast,
and opened up a tin of sardines.

After they were finished eating, Mr. Tumnus began playing music on a strange little flute.

Lucy began to get sleepy.
Then the music made Lucy fall fast asleep.

When Lucy woke,
Mr. Tumnus looked nervous.
"I am a terrible Faun," he said.
Then he told Lucy that he had planned
to turn her over to the White Witch.

"It is because of the White Witch
that it is so cold in Narnia.
She cast a spell that turned Narnia cold
for one hundred years!" Mr. Tumnus said.

"If anyone ever finds a Human in the woods,
he must turn it over to her,"
Mr. Tumnus explained.
"If he does not, she will turn him to stone!"
Mr. Tumnus told Lucy that only Humans have
the power to break the White Witch's spell
and end the long winter.
If that happens, the White Witch will lose her
control over Narnia!

Mr. Tumnus looked sadly at his new friend.
He knew he ought to give her to the Witch.
What have I done? he thought.
Then Mr. Tumnus had a change of heart.
He could not send Lucy to the White Witch.
"Come on! We do not have much time!"
he cried.

Mr. Tumnus and Lucy raced
back to the lamppost.
Mr. Tumnus's eyes filled with tears
as he said good-bye.
He knew it was for the best—
if Lucy did not leave now,
the White Witch would take her.
"No matter what happens," he said,
"you have made me feel warmer
than I have in one hundred years."
Waving a last good-bye,
Lucy made her way back
through the wardrobe.

Home safely, Lucy could hardly believe
her strange adventure in Narnia.
But she knew in her heart she would see
her friend Mr. Tumnus again.